FRUIT Fables

Sir Beaver Finds the Missing *Peace*

Shelleen Weaver

Haste Laud PRESS

illustrated by Cody Wood

Once upon a winding creek,

where brook trout swim and bullfrogs leap,

Sir Beaver lived, but couldn't sleep

nor leave his work for fun.

He didn't have a moment's peace
but worked and worried frantically,
buzz-sawing wood with big front teeth
from dawn 'til setting sun.

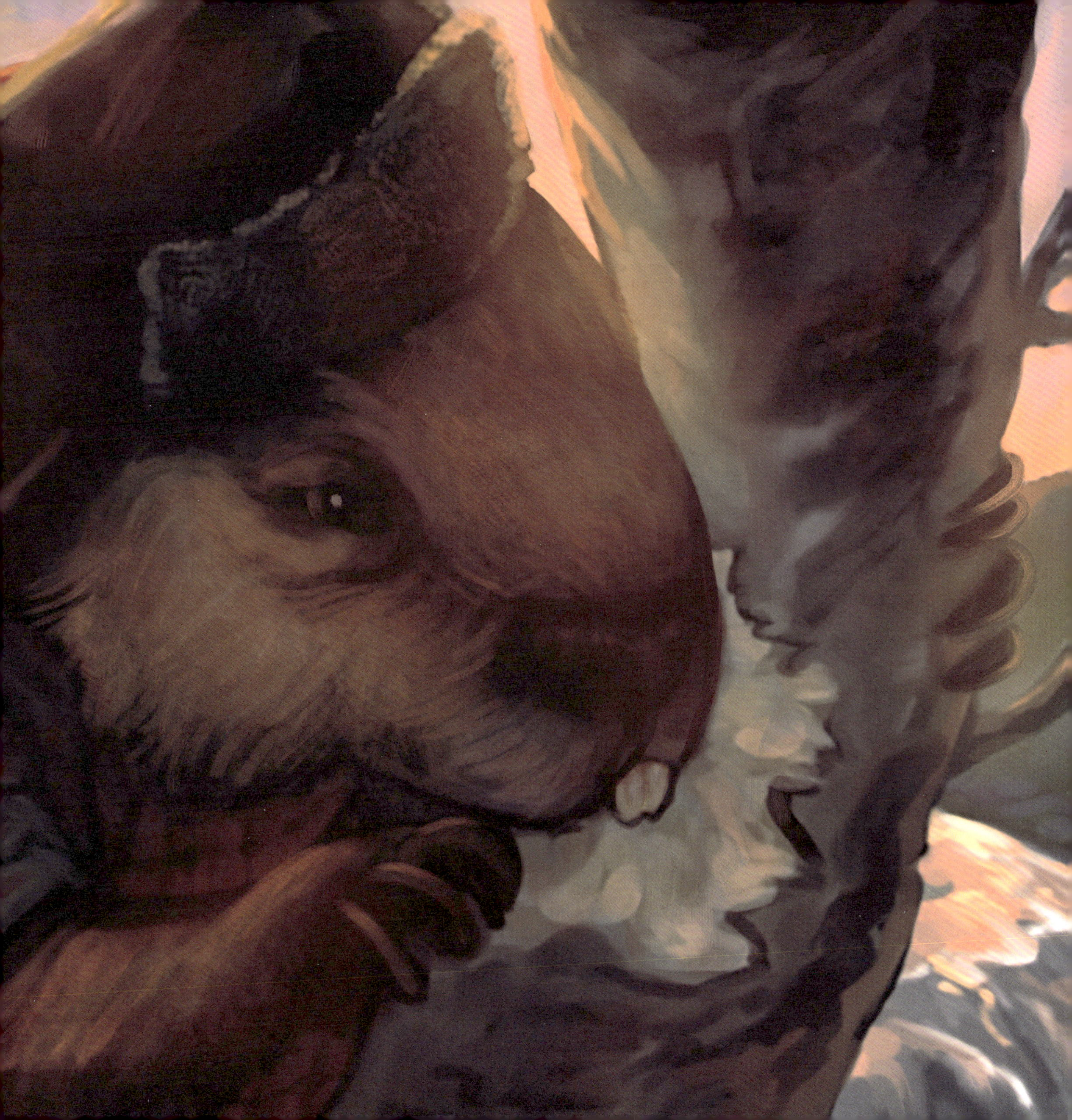

Those around were working too.

The squirrels were packing in their food.

Caterpillars spun cocoons.

Young birds tried to fly.

Nectar sipped from blossomed flowers,
ants that marched from hour to hour–
all with glee– no moods were sour,
and Beav did not know why!

Sometimes when squirrels would stop to play,
or otters swam or napped in shade,
or deer would rest in beds they made,
Sir Beav would fret and fuss.

"There is no time to rest or play,
for winter looms. It's on its way.
We all must work and not delay!"
His tail smacked his disgust.

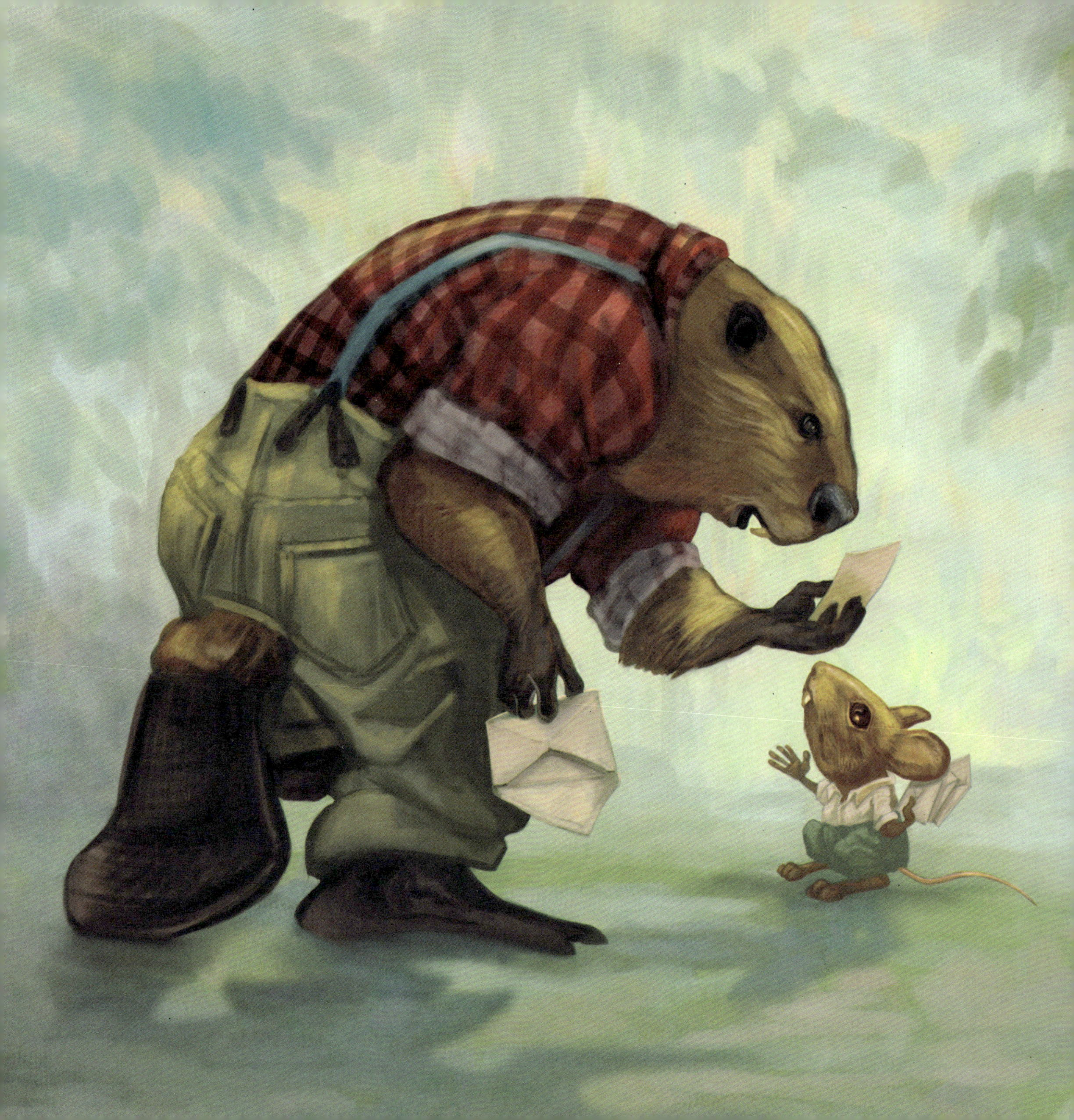

"Hey, Beav," chim-chimed a small field mouse,
"Take a break from your mud-stick house.
Tonight, we feast with Polly Grouse.
Won't you be our guest?"

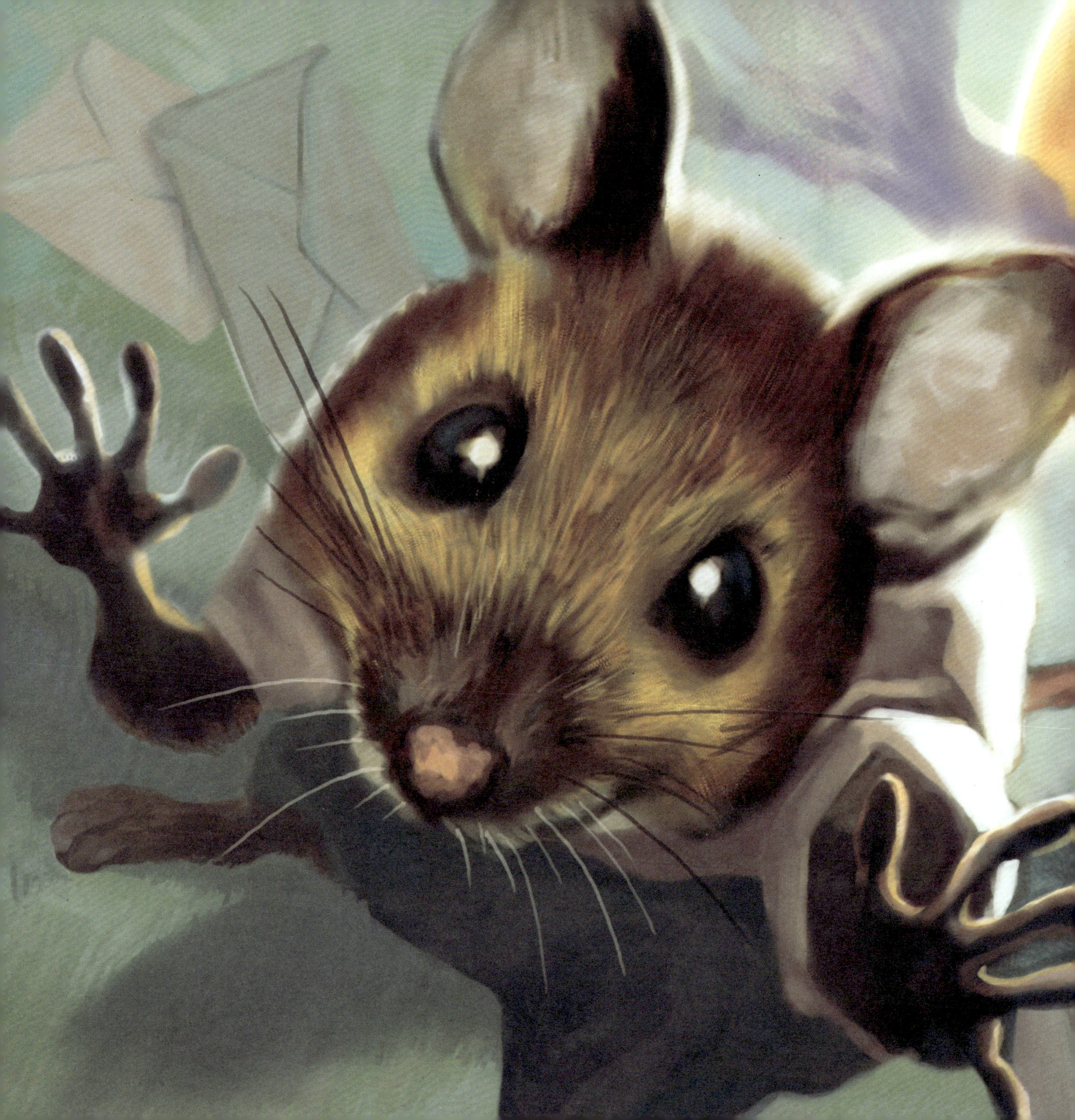

"We'll celebrate 'neath harvest moon.
We'll dance as peepers flute their tune,
and feast on our abundant food.
It's time for thanks and rest."

"Oh no," Beav sighed. "That just won't do."
His heart beat fast as tension grew.
"I must work-work. No time to lose.
I'm sorry. I must run!"

But as he worked that afternoon,
he got an ache in his front tooth.
It hurt to saw and hurt to chew.
How would his work be done?

And so he stopped where deer had made
a bed where fir trees gave their shade
and thought, "This really does feel great!
I could get used to this."

And then he heard a happy song.
His beaver toe tap-tapped along.
It was the party going on—
the one he'd planned to miss.

A sweet aroma whiffed his nose,
and from his gut a gurgle rose.
"I could visit, I suppose,"
he thought with sheepish grin.

Imagine all of their surprise—
delighted looks lit up the eyes
of deer, the birds, the squirrels, and mice,
when he walked up to them.

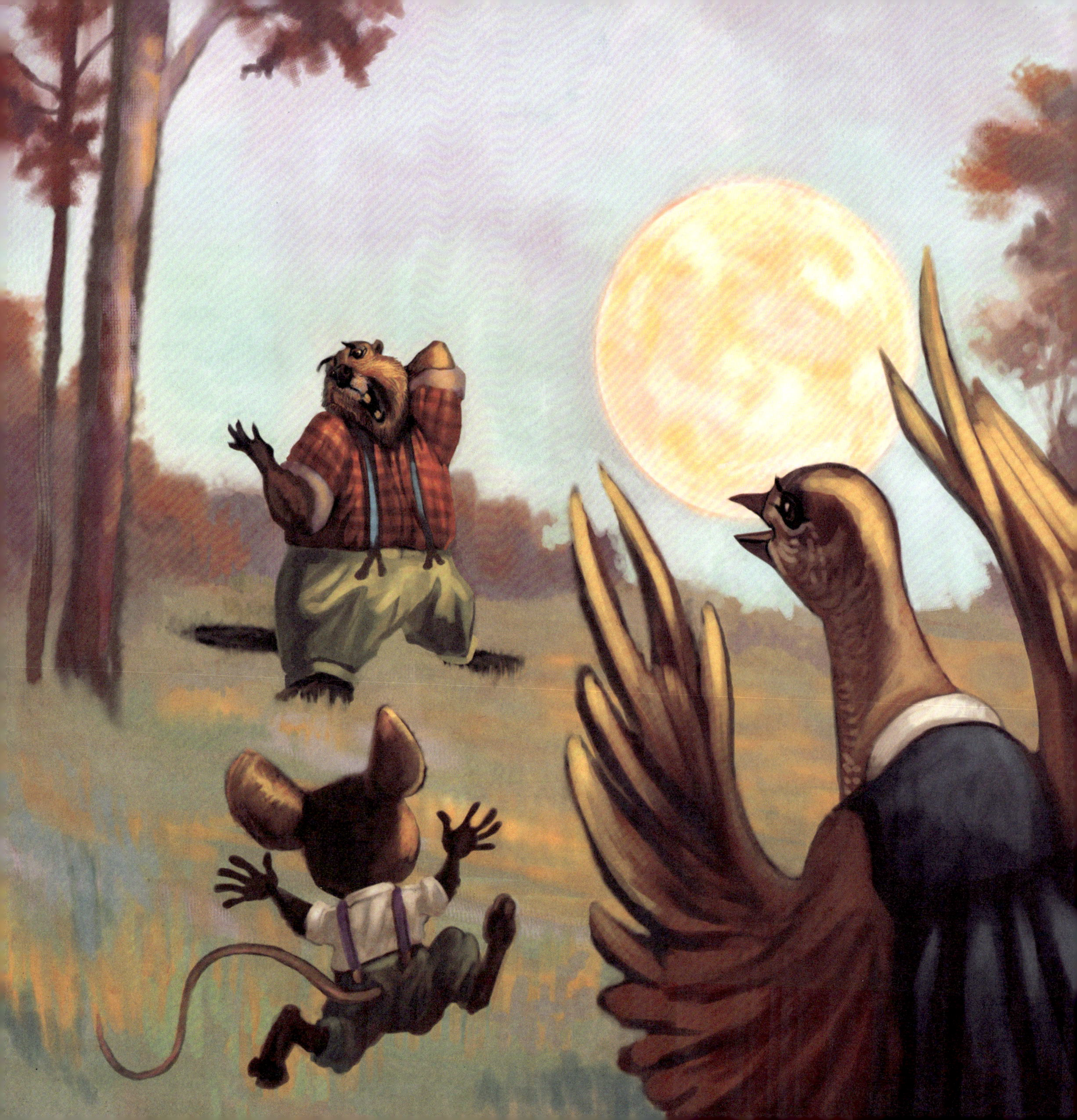

He joined the feast that had begun.
They told him they were glad he'd come.
And for a time, Sir Beav had fun,
despite his tooth that throbbed.

They sang a song at party's end.
Then Beav began to fret again.
"It's late in fall. My walls are thin!"
he told his friends through sobs.

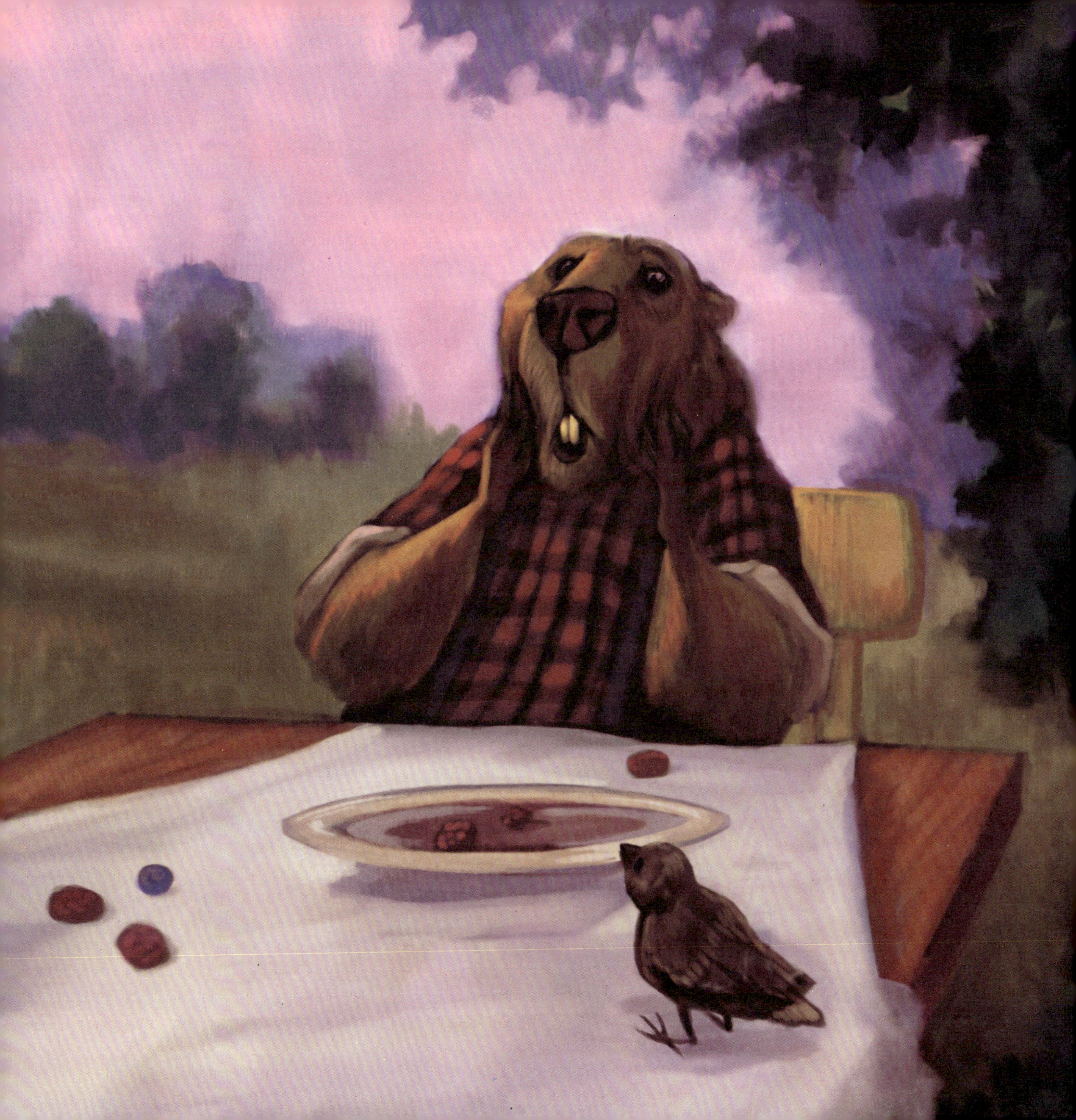

Field mouse smiled and made a squeak,
"Let's take a walk. That's what you need.
I'll help you find the missing *peace*.
Let's go and get some air."

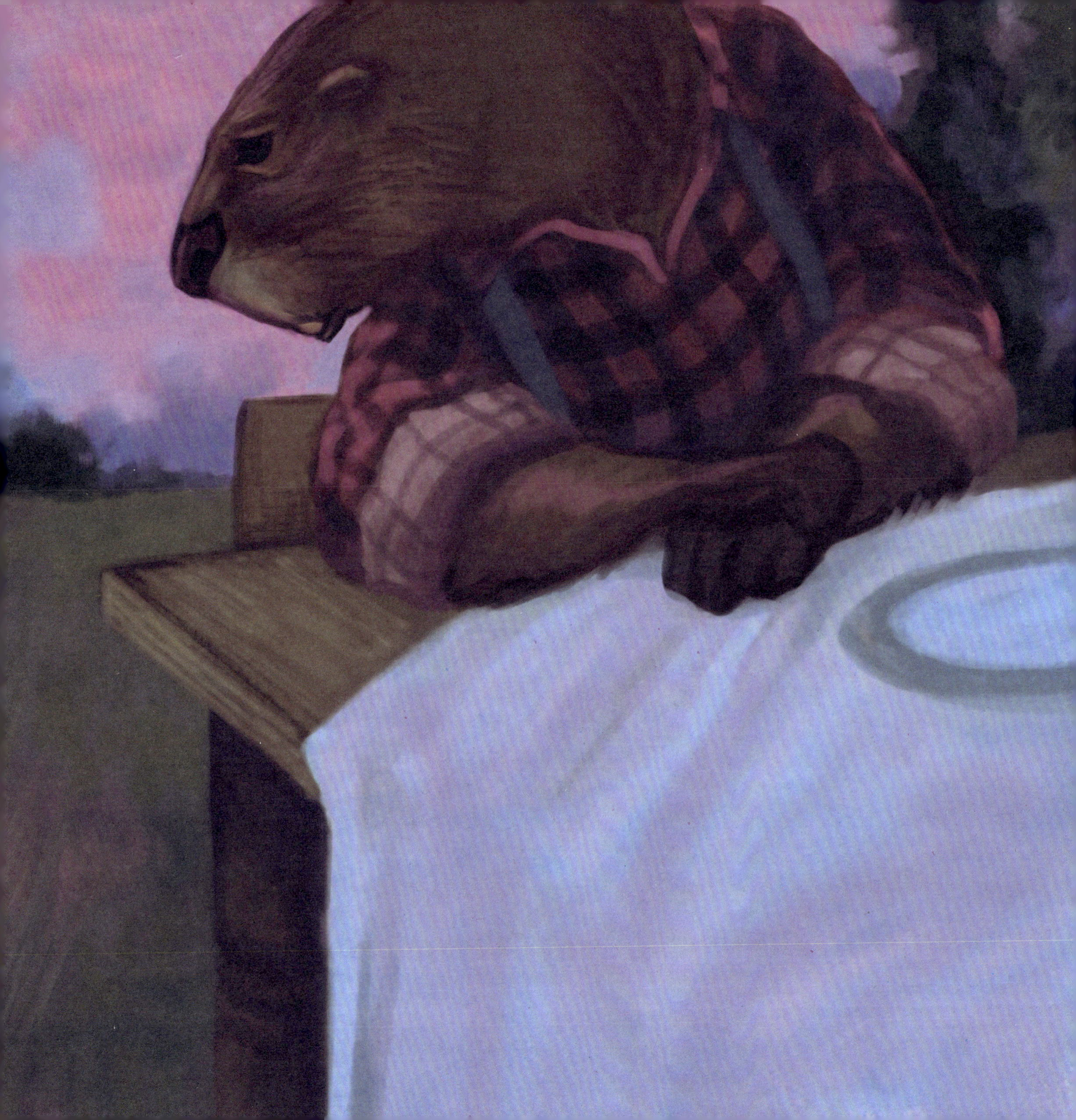

"Working hard is good," he said.
"But so is play and rest in bed.
Worry will upset your head.
You must cast your cares."

"We all work hard, it's plain to see,
but we can do it merrily,
because we trust that all our needs,
our Maker will provide."

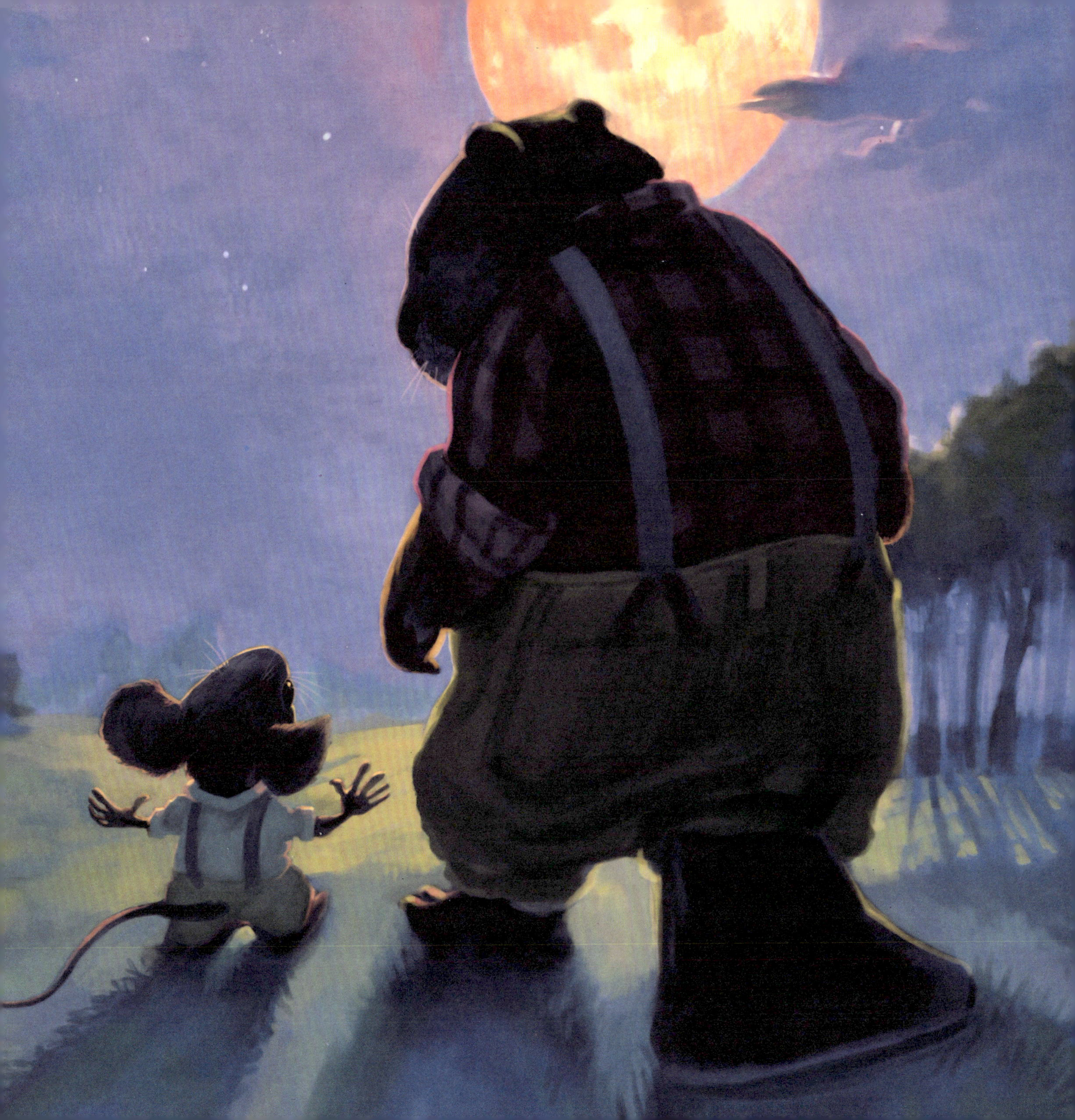

"Peace comes when we do our best
and trust that God provides the rest.
Just look around at how we're blessed
and celebrate tonight!"

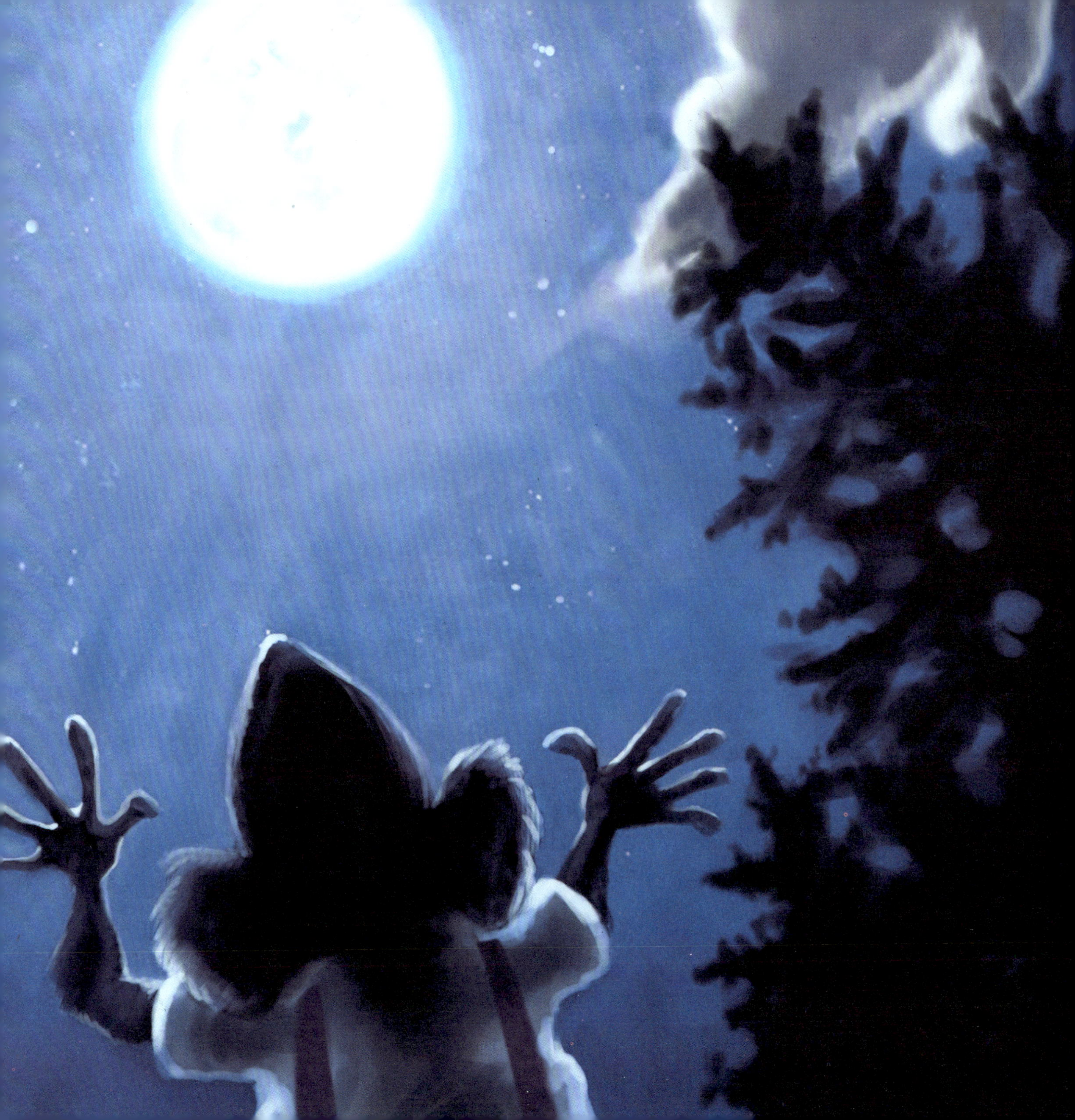

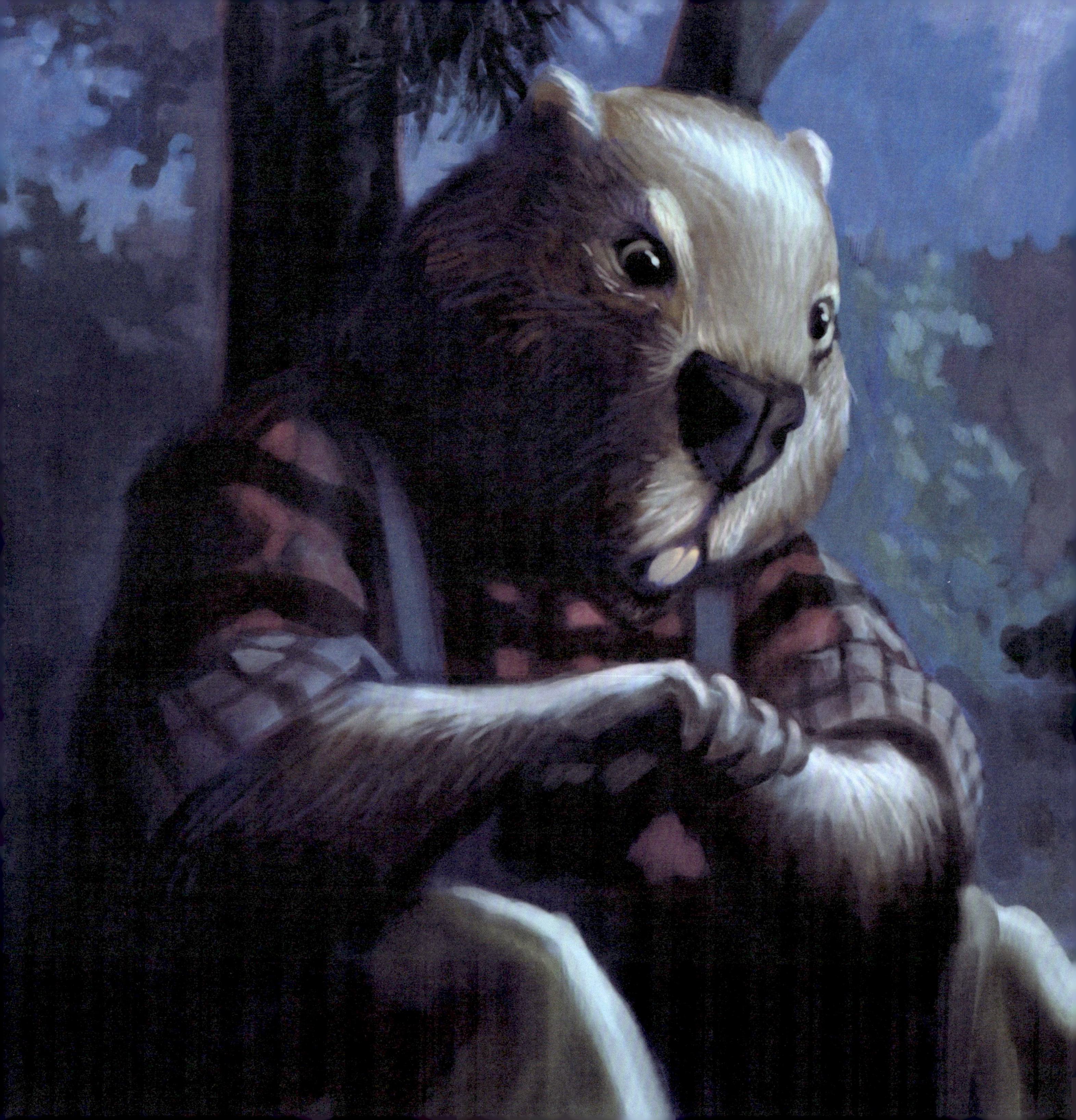

Sir Beav looked down at his fur coat
that kept him warm in winter's cold,
as worry lines, etched deep from growth,
began to melt away.

And so, Sir Beav, that very day,
chose to throw his fear away,
and found the peace from God who made
all creatures small and great.

Let's Chew on It...

Was Sir Beaver the only one preparing for winter in this story?

Why didn't Sir Beaver want to go to the harvest party?

What made Sir Beaver stop working?

What did Field Mouse mean when he told Sir Beaver that he must cast his cares?

Who is Sir Beaver's Maker, and what did He give Sir Beaver to help keep him warm?

After his tooth heals, do you think Sir Beaver will go back to working on his house?

Do you think that Sir Beaver will worry less and play more too?

This story is about peace. Peace is one of the fruits or behaviors we learn from God's Holy Spirit. Let's say our theme verse together:

"...the fruit of the spirit is love, joy, peace, patience, kindness, goodness, faithfulness, gentleness, [and] self-control..."

— Galatians 5:22-23 NASB

Prayer:

Dear Heavenly Father,

Thank you for giving us the fruit of your Spirit. Please fill us with your peace.

We pray in Jesus' name,
— Amen

Dear Parents, Teachers, and Loved Ones,

Thank you for purchasing this book. Did you and your children enjoy it? I would love to hear from you. I read and respond to every email. You can contact me at: **ShelleenWeaver.com.**

There you can also find updates on my latest projects, fun freebies, and more. *Visit soon!*

Come meet us - myself and the illustrator, that is. Cody and I teamed up to bring your children a read-aloud version of this story.
We also unpack "Let's Chew On It!" and sing a theme song at the end.
Join the fun on this book's page at:
ShelleenWeaver.com.

One more thing: If you see value in this book series, would you help spread the word? Reviews are vital to authors. They help us publish and sell more books. If you purchased this book online, would you consider posting a review there? Sharing on social media or telling a friend is also very helpful. I would be grateful.

May God bless you as you train up your treasures in the way they should go.
I'm honored to be a part of your journey.

With love,

Shelleen Weaver

P.S. There's more to come in the Fruit Fables collection!
   Visit **ShelleenWeaver.com** for publishing updates.

About the Author

Shelleen Weaver is a poet, former Miss Teen of Pennsylvania, singer/songwriter/recording artist of the CRW #1 hit song, *Enraptured*, a speaker, wife, and mom...

... and completely, utterly, a child at heart.

The Fruit Fables series grew out of bedtime stories and original lullabies she told and sang to her children when they were young. Shelleen lives with her husband and three children in gorgeous Lancaster County, Pennsylvania.

More at **ShelleenWeaver.com**

About the Illustrator

Like many visual artists, Cody Wood has drawn pictures for as long as he can remember. A framed piece of his art still hangs in the elementary school of his childhood. As an animator, his work has been featured in national TV ads and on Cartoon Network. Despite a career in the visual arts, Fruit Fables is his first venture into book illustration.

Cody has also spent time as a worship leader and student ministry director. He lives in Columbus, Ohio with his wife and two sons.